MICHAEL

Padd

in the KITCHEN
Illustrated by Barry Wilkinson

COLLINS COLOUR CUBS

One morning, Mr. and Mrs. Brown woke feeling ill . . . so they went straight back to bed.

"The trouble is," said Mrs. Brown, "with Jonathan and Judy at school and Mrs. Bird on holiday, who's going to look after us?"

"Don't worry, Mrs. Brown," exclaimed Paddington. "I'll do it! Bears are good at looking after people."

"I'll make you a stew," he announced, as he left the room. "Aunt Lucy always made me a stew when I wasn't well."

"Oh, dear!" groaned Mr. Brown. "I think I suddenly feel worse again!"

Paddington hurried downstairs as fast as his legs would carry him. He was very keen on cooking; at least, he always felt he would be if he ever got the chance.

He'd often watched Mrs. Bird at work in her kitchen and although he'd never actually made a stew himself before, she always made it look very easy. He couldn't wait to have a go.

First of all, he cut up some meat and
put it into a saucepan.

Then he added a pawful of carrots, some water and several onions for good measure.

After he'd put the saucepan on the stove to boil, Paddington turned his attention to the important matter of the dumplings.

Mrs. Bird made very good stews. If he had any complaints at all it was that her dumplings were a little on the small side.

Paddington decided that *his* dumplings
would be the biggest ever made.

It was some while before the cloud of flour finally settled, but when it had, he added a generous helping of suet . . .

. . . followed by a jug of milk.

It was when he came to stir the mixture that Paddington first began to feel worried. The spoon went into the bowl easily enough . . .

. . . but once in, it didn't seem to want to move.

In fact, far from being able to *stir* the mixture, Paddington began to wonder if he would ever get the spoon out again.

He didn't remember Mrs. Bird having so much trouble with *her* dumplings and he began to wish he'd consulted one of her recipe books first.

Paddington decided to make the best of a bad job. He took the saucepan of stew off the stove and tried to empty his dumpling mixture into it.

But the bowl was a lot heavier than he'd expected . . .

. . . and no matter how hard he shook it, nothing seemed to happen.

He decided the only thing to do
was give the basin a sharp tap with
Mrs. Bird's rolling pin.

But he soon wished he hadn't.

For a moment, Paddington toyed
with the idea of hollowing out the
dumpling mixture and making it into
a new basin to replace the one he'd
broken, but matters were suddenly decided
for him . . .

. . . as the lump of dough slid into the stew with a loud "plop".

But Paddington's troubles weren't over
by a long way. Far from it being *in*
the saucepan, half the dumpling mixture
was sticking out of the top. And for
some strange reason it seemed to be
growing larger with every passing
moment.

In fact, it had grown so much even his hat wasn't big enough to take it all.

In the end, Paddington decided to do what Mr. Brown always did with the family suitcase when they went on holiday . . .

. . . he stood on the lid!

The saucepan was now so heavy Paddington wasn't at all sure how he managed to get it back on to the stove, but he was so worn out he didn't really care.

After mopping his brow with a tea towel, he sat down in the middle of the kitchen floor and closed his eyes. A few seconds later some loud snores added themselves to the sound of bubbling stew.

Paddington wasn't sure how long he slept, but he woke with a nasty feeling that he wasn't alone. SOME-THING was in the room with him and it was getting nearer . . . and nearer.

Just as he began to think that perhaps he was in the middle of a nightmare, there was a loud crash from the direction of the stove and something rolled across the floor towards him.

Paddington was a brave bear at heart, but he didn't stay to see what it was. Instead, he beat a hasty retreat in the direction of the garden.

He felt it would be better to investigate
the matter from the other side of the
window.

It wasn't until much later that morning that Mr. Brown happened to look out of the bedroom window. As he did so he gave a start.

"That's funny," he exclaimed. "There's a big white thing in the garden. Come and have a look. I'm sure it wasn't there just now."

Mrs. Brown joined her husband at the window. Sure enough, standing in the middle of the rockery, was a large, white object.

"Whatever can it be, Henry?" she asked.

"Do *you* know what it is, Paddington?" asked Mr. Brown, as the door opened and a small figure in a duffle coat came into the room carrying a tray laden with food.

"Perhaps it's a snowball, Mr. Brown,"
said Paddington innocently.

"In midsummer!" exclaimed Mrs.
Brown.

"Well, whatever it is," said Mr. Brown, "those birds don't seem to think much of it. I think one of them has just broken its beak."

"In that case," said Paddington hastily, as he placed the tray between the two beds, "I think you should hurry up and eat yours before it sets!"

Mr. and Mrs. Brown exchanged glances.
"Before it *sets*!" repeated Mr. Brown.
"I don't like the sound of that!"

"Neither do I," agreed Mrs. Brown
nervously.

"Well," said Paddington, playing for time while the others got back into bed. "I'm afraid I've been having trouble with my dumplings, but don't worry . . . I've got some spare mixture. It's under my . . . Oh! Oh, dear!"

"*Now* what's the matter?" asked Mr. Brown. For some strange reason, Paddington seemed to be having trouble taking his hat off.

"Well," gasped Paddington, "you may want some 'seconds', Mr. Brown, and I wouldn't want to disappoint you.

"There's nothing worse than being without dumplings.

"Especially when you're ill!"

This story comes from PADDINGTON HELPS OUT
and is based on the television film. It has been
specially written by Michael Bond for
younger children.

ISBN 0 00 123208 8 (paperback)
ISBN 0 00 123215 0 (cased)
Text copyright © 1977 Michael Bond
Illustrations copyright © 1977 William Collins Sons & Co. Ltd.
Cover copyright © 1977 William Collins Sons & Co. Ltd. and Film Fair Ltd.
Cover design by Ivor Wood. Cover photographed by Bruce Scott.
Printed in Great Britain